MEGAZORD
TO THE RESCUE!

By Cathy East Dubowski

A PARACHUTE PRESS BOOK

A PARACHUTE PRESS BOOK
Parachute Press, Inc.
156 Fifth Avenue
New York, NY 10010

Creative Consultant: Cheryl Saban

With special thanks to Cheryl Saban, Sheila Dennen, Debi Young, and
Sherry Stack.

Printed in the U.S.A.
May 1994
ISBN: 0-938753-79-7
  B C D E F G H I J

The Battle Begins

Long ago, Good and Evil met in a great battle. The wizard Zordon led the forces of Good. He fought against Rita Repulsa, who wanted to rule the universe with her forces of Evil.

Both sides fought hard, but the war ended in a tie. So Zordon and

Rita made a deal. They would both flip coins to decide who was the winner. Whoever made the best three tosses out of five would win. The loser would be locked away forever.

Of course, Zordon did not want to risk the safety of the universe on five coins—unless they were magic coins! So with his five special coins, Zordon won the coin toss. But Rita had one last trick up her sleeve. Before she was locked away, she trapped Zordon in another dimension. Now he must stay inside a column of green light at his command center forever and ever.

Rita and her wicked friends

were dropped into an intergalactic prison and flung through space. They crashed into a tiny moon of a faraway planet. After ten thousand years, space travelers found the prison and opened it. Rita and her servants, Baboo, Squatt, Goldar, and Finster, were free!

Rita hadn't changed one bit in ten thousand years. She began planning to take over the universe again. And she saw her first target in the sky above—Earth!

When Zordon heard of Rita's escape, he put his master plan into action. He called Alpha 5, the robot running his command center on Earth. "Teleport to us five of the wildest, most willful humans in the area," he commanded.

"No!" Alpha 5 said. "Not... teenagers!"

But Alpha 5 did as he was told, and teleported five teenagers to the command center.

"Earth is under attack by the evil Rita Repulsa," Zordon explained to the teenagers. "I have chosen you to battle her and save the planet. Each of you will receive great powers drawn from the spirits of the dinosaurs."

Zordon gave each teenager a belt with a magic coin—a Power Morpher! "When you are in danger, raise your Power Morpher to

4

the sky," Zordon instructed. "Then call out the name of your dinosaur and you will morph into a mighty fighter—a Power Ranger!

"Jason, you will be the Red Ranger, with the power of the great tyrannosaurus," Zordon explained. "Trini will be the Yellow Ranger, with the force of the saber-toothed tiger. Zack will be the Black Ranger, with the power of the mastodon. Kimberly will be the Pink Ranger, with pterodactyl power. And Billy will be the Blue Ranger, backed by the power of the triceratops."

For big problems, the Power Rangers could call upon Dinozords—giant robots they piloted into battle. And if things got really tough, the Dinozords could combine together to make a super-robot—a mighty Megazord!

Power Rangers, dinosaur spirits, and robots—together, these incredible forces would protect the Earth.

But the teenagers had to follow Zordon's three rules:

1. Never use your powers for selfish reasons.

2. Never make a fight worse—unless Rita forces you.

3. Always keep your identities secret. No one must ever find out that you are a Mighty Morphin Power Ranger!

CHAPTER 1

It was Monday morning in Ms. Appleby's science class. Video projects were due.

Near the front of the room, five friends talked about their projects. They looked like ordinary kids. They weren't. In fact, *they* would make a good science project themselves—if their classmates only knew!

Jason, Kimberly, Zack, Billy, and Trini had secret powers. Whenever danger threatened, they changed into the Mighty Morphin Power Rangers!

This morning, though, they were just typical students. As the final class bell rang, Ms. Appleby folded her hands on her plump middle and smiled. "Good morning, class. I—"

Crash! The classroom door banged open. Two students burst into the room. One was nearly as wide as the door. The other one was skinny and holding a camera to his face. They were still filming their video!

The skinny kid aimed his camera at the big one and said, "*Bulk, the World's Greatest Guy,* scene 32."

Bulk gave the camera a fake movie-star smile. "I have always enjoyed this wonderful class . . ."

Their teacher frowned. "Bulk! Skull! Please take your seats!"

"That's Ms. Appleby," Bulk said to the camera. "She can't wait for me to sit down. She really is a lovely teacher."

Bulk backed up to his desk. But he was too busy smiling into the camera to watch where he was going. When he sat down, he missed his chair completely and crashed to the floor.

Skull's camera was still recording. Bulk shook his fist.

"Don't worry," said Skull. "I'll just cut that part."

Ms. Appleby glared at the two boys, then shook her head and sighed. "Now," she said to the class, "it's time for our video projects. Trini, would you go first, please?"

Tall, willowy Trini walked gracefully to the front of the room. She popped her tape into the VCR. Then she flipped her long black hair over her shoulder as she faced the class. "My video project is called *Pollution Problems in Angel Grove.*"

A close-up of Trini's face appeared on the TV screen: *"A lot has been done to clean up the environment in the past few years. But pollution is still a problem. Even here in beautiful Angel Grove."*

Trini's classmates stared in surprise at the pictures she had recorded. Scenes of parks littered with soda cans and fast-food wrappers. Factories belching thick black smoke. Lakes choked with grunge and garbage.

Jason shook his head. "This is totally terrible."

Even Zack, who was usually cracking jokes, watched silently.

Trini's voice concluded the video. *"If we destroy nature, the animals will disappear. And if the animals disappear, we will, too. The time to act is now."*

The whole class broke into applause.

"Very nice job, Trini," said Ms. Appleby. "Pollution is a serious concern for our society."

"Awesome video!" Kimberly said as Trini took her seat. "What can we do to make things better in Angel Grove?"

"I have an idea," Trini said with an eager smile. "I want to start a Clean-Up Club. Each week we can do some recycling, clean up nature trails, or find ways to save endangered animals."

"Count me in!" said Jason.

"Sounds cool!" Zack agreed.

Full of ideas, the five Power Rangers began to make plans.

Someone was watching them.

Someone who hated them and everything they stood for.

Her name was Rita Repulsa. She looked through her magic telescope from the balcony of her cold dark fortress on the moon. "I'll stop their silly cleanup!" she told Goldar and Scorpina, her two warriors. "My new weapon will ruin their whole stupid planet!"

Rita threw her head back and laughed. "It will make their environment so polluted, they'll *never* be able to clean it up!"

CHAPTER 2

Tall, handsome Jason studied his opponent. Then, with smooth, practiced moves, he leaped forward.

"Hiii-yaah!"

Jason's hand sliced down on his target.

Crunch!

Trini's started a new club—the Clean-Up Club!

Bulk and Skull pretend they want to help with the recycling drive.

The Power Rangers are ready to work hard to clean up the field.

The Putty Patrol stops the cleanup!

Kimberly trashes some Putties!

Pow! Trini's quick moves keep a Putty away.

Trini and Billy enjoy a peaceful moment—now that the Putties are gone!

On the viewing globe, the Power Rangers watch Rita's Polluticorn attack the recycling center.

The air crackles with electricity as the Power Rangers teleport back to Earth.

Trini and Kimberly are ready to morph!

"Need some help, Polluticorn?" asks
Goldar.

Rita's warrior Scorpina gets a Power Ranger punch!

The Power Rangers return to being regular kids—with a big secret!

"Cool!" said Zack as Jason flattened one more aluminum can. They were recycling cans at the Angel Grove Youth Center.

"How's it going?" asked Trini. She and the Power Rangers were wearing their new green Clean-Up Club T-shirts.

"Great," said Zack. "Two more cans and we're done."

"Good going, guys," she said. Then Trini joined Billy and Kimberly. They were helping Ernie, the juice bar owner, set up recycling bins. Billy had used organic paint to label each bin: Glass, Aluminum Cans, and Plastic. He wanted to make sure the bins were organized.

Kimberly wanted to make sure they looked good! "Okay—a little to the left," she told Ernie.

He moved the bins left.

"Hmm." Kimberly twirled a strand of her shoulder-length brown hair. "Back a little to the right," she said.

Ernie moved the bins right.

"Perfect!" Kimberly said.

When the Power Rangers finished their work, Ernie said, "Hey, you guys. Thanks for helping me out with all this recycling stuff."

"No problem," said Trini. She looked around at her friends. "Are we ready to tackle the field near the park?"

"You bet," said Jason. "Let's go."

When the Power Rangers arrived at the field, they couldn't believe what they found. Old tires, bottles and cans, and newspapers covered the grass.

"This is terrible," said Jason.

"I wish people would throw their trash in the cans," said Kimberly.

Trini said, "It's time to take back the field." She held up some extra-large trash bags. "Clean-Up Club to the rescue!"

So Jason, Kimberly, Zack, Trini, and Billy began to clean up — Power Ranger style!

They crisscrossed the field doing back flips and cartwheels, picking up trash as they went.

Zack danced some hip-hop moves across the field. Then he stashed his trash as if he were slam-dunking a basketball into Billy's bag.

"This is morphinominal!" he shouted.

Working together, they soon had a mountain of trash bags.

"Looks like our club is really cleaning up," said Jason.

"And it's fun, too," added Zack.

"Now let's do that last section over there," said Trini.

"Now let's do that section over there," Rita cackled, imitating Trini. "I can't wait to send my secret weapon," she told Goldar as they watched the Clean-Up Club at work. "It will destroy the Power Rangers so I can take over the Earth!"

"Another brilliant plan, Your Badness," said Goldar.

"But first," Rita said, "I'll send the Putties to tire them out!"

Back in the field, the Clean-Up Club was still picking up litter. Trini wrinkled her nose as she stashed a plate full of rotten food in a bag. "That's the last of it," she said.

Suddenly they heard a gurgling sound somewhere behind them.

Then another. Then more!

"What's that noise?" asked Kimberly. Her brown eyes looked worried.

Billy pointed to the edge of the field. "It's Rita's Putty Patrol!"

"I wonder what Rita's trying to do this time?" Jason said.

Dozens of the mindless clay fighters now appeared. Suddenly they surrounded the Power Rangers.

"Man!" said Zack. "Now we've got something else to clean up."

Zack spun in a circle, knocking six Putties to the ground.

Two Putties closed in on Kimberly, but she sprang into the air. The Putties crashed heads and knocked each other out.

The teens used karate, gymnastic moves, and teamwork to block the Putties' attacks.

Then suddenly, mysteriously, the Putties vanished.

The kids looked around, gasping for breath. They checked to make sure everyone was okay.

"Whew," said Zack. "Trashing those Putties is a big help to our environment."

That made everybody laugh. But not for long.

Moments later a horrible roar split the air.

"What's that?" cried Trini.

The Power Rangers looked up. They had never seen anything like the monster that filled the sky.

It was as tall as a huge man. It had the face of a horse and a long black mane. Its body was covered with gray armorlike skin. Jutting up from its head was one white horn.

It flew on huge powerful wings, straight toward the Power Rangers!

Zack jumped to his feet. "Yo, monster horse, sky high!"

"And it's flying in fast!" cried Kimberly.

Jason knew it would take more than a few karate kicks to stop this monster. "It's morphin time!" he shouted to his friends.

The air crackled sharply with

electricity as they raised their Power Morphers to the sky. As Zordon had taught them, they called upon the spirits of the ancient dinosaurs.

"Mastodon!" cried Zack.

"Pterodactyl!" cried Kimberly.

"Triceratops!" cried Billy.

"Saber-toothed Tiger!" cried Trini.

"Tyrannosaurus!" cried Jason.

In a flash, the five morphed into—Power Rangers!

Now they stood dressed in sleek jumpsuits and shining helmets. Jason the Red Ranger. Kimberly the Pink Ranger. Zack the Black Ranger. Trini the Yellow Ranger. And Billy the Blue Ranger.

The Power Rangers locked hands, uniting their strength. Then together they faced their new foe.

With an unearthly roar, the horse monster flew right between them, knocking them all to the ground.

Dazed, Jason and Zack pulled themselves to their knees.

"Let's get him!" cried Jason.

They ran toward the monster. It let out a horrible laugh. Then it blasted them with its magic horn.

Before they could recover, the horse began to flap its huge scary wings. "Power wings, blow!" it roared.

The wind was as strong as a

tornado. It tossed Zack and Jason through the air. They landed in a red and black heap.

"You guys okay?" Trini asked as she helped Zack to his feet.

"Come on," said Kimberly. "We've got to stop this thing!"

The Power Rangers charged the monster again and again. But nothing worked.

"It doesn't even feel our attacks!" Billy cried.

Lightning flashed from its glowing horn. "I am the Polluticorn," the beast cried. "And I will destroy you and your miserable planet!"

CHAPTER 4

The Polluticorn struck. But nothing was there!

Five balls of sparkling colored light—red, pink, black, yellow, and blue—streaked across the sky, into a building hidden in the hot sands.

Inside this secret compound,

the lights sparkled and Jason, Trini, Kimberly, Zack, and Billy appeared. They were surrounded by computers and blinking lights.

This was the command center of Zordon, who had given them their powers. He had pulled them from the battle just in time.

The Power Rangers waited. Soon Zordon's pale face wavered in a column of eerie green light.

"Zordon," said Jason. "This horse monster is awesome."

Zordon's image nodded. "It will be difficult to defeat this new monster Rita has created. Billy, please help Alpha 5 with a battle plan while I brief the others."

Billy walked over to a small

robot working the controls. Red lights blinked around the rim of its metal head.

"So what's the story on this new monster, Zordon?" Zack asked.

"It's Rita's latest plan to destroy the Earth," Zordon answered. "Look at the viewing globe."

The kids gathered around the globe as an image of the winged horse appeared.

"Rita created the Polluticorn to wipe out the planet with pollution," said Zordon.

"There's got to be a way to stop that thing," said Jason.

"But how?" Kimberly asked.

"Aye-yi-yi-yi-yi!" Alpha 5 was

spinning in circles, tangling himself in the long computer printout. With a squeak, he crashed to the floor. The Power Rangers ran over to help.

Billy read a piece of the printout. "My analysis shows that the Polluticorn derives its power from its horn."

"Good work," said Zordon.

Suddenly an alarm sounded. Zordon frowned. He knew what that meant. The Polluticorn was attacking again. On the viewing globe, the Power Rangers saw the Angel Grove Recycling Center.

Workers ran from the building as the Polluticorn blasted it with its horn.

"We can't let him wreck the recycling center!" said Trini.

Jason nodded. "It's morphin time again!"

Once more, the Power Rangers raised their Power Morphers in the air. They called on the powers of the ancient dinosaurs. "Mastodon!" "Pterodactyl!" "Triceratops!" "Saber-toothed Tiger!" "Tyrannosaurus!" A crackling glow filled the command center.

"POWER RANGERS!" the five shouted.

The Power Rangers morphed and began to fade, back to their fight with the Polluticorn.

CHAPTER 5

Seconds later the Power Rangers materialized at the Angel Grove Recycling Center. With new determination, they faced the Polluticorn.

Just as they were about to charge, Goldar and Scorpina, Rita's two evil warriors, appeared, blocking their path.

"Now what?" said Billy.

"You guys get them," said Jason. "I'll get horn head!"

Jason quickly went after the Polluticorn. At first the two enemies seemed closely matched—until a blast from the monster's horn slammed Jason to the ground. Facedown in the dirt, he gasped, "I've got to...find a way...to chop off that horn!"

"I'm just too powerful for you, puny ranger!" the Polluticorn roared. "I'm going to finish destroying this recycling center. You'll never clean up this stupid planet!"

Jason was back on his feet.

"Your polluting days are over, Horseface. I'm sending you back to the barn!"

A cry for help stopped Jason in his tracks.

"Jason," shouted Zack. "Help!" It was a word Zack rarely used. Jason looked around. Goldar and Scorpina had knocked the others to the ground. Their swords were ready to strike his friends.

"I summon the power of the Dragon Shield!" Jason cried. A collar of shining gold appeared on Jason's shoulders. He held his sword in one hand.

The Polluticorn stood between Jason and his friends. Again Jason charged. Again the Polluticorn blasted him with its horn. But the blows just bounced off the Dragon Shield.

Jason sprang as high as he could and raised his sword. Then he swung the blade down with all his might. And the Polluticorn's horn lay smoking on the ground.

The monster grabbed its head. "My horn!" it roared.

Jason brought his sword down again, knocking Goldar and Scorpina's blades to the ground.

High above Earth Rita saw the Polluticorn's horn lying in the dirt. "I'll get you for that!" she screamed. She raised her magic staff and hurled it toward Earth. "See the Polluticorn grow!"

Rita's staff rocketed to the planet below. The ground shook. Lightning flashed from the staff, snaking its way to the Polluticorn.

Before the Power Rangers could attack again, the Polluticorn began to grow taller and taller until it towered over the tallest buildings in Angel Grove.

The Power Rangers stared up at the giant horse monster. "We need Dinozord Power now! Tyrannosaurus!" Jason cried, raising a fist into the air.

"Mastodon!" cried Zack.

"Pterodactyl!" cried Kimberly.

"Triceratops!" cried Billy.

"Saber-toothed Tiger!" cried Trini.

The ground trembled from the distant sound of dinosaur robots awakening.

Tyrannosaurus erupted from a steaming crack in the ground.

Mastodon broke through its cage of ice.

Triceratops charged across a steaming desert.

Saber-toothed Tiger leaped through a twisted jungle.

Pterodactyl erupted from the fires of a volcano.

Side by side they raced like the wind to answer the call.

The Power Rangers leaped into the cockpits of their Zords.

"Is everybody ready?" Jason shouted.

"READY!" the Power Rangers answered.

"Okay," said Jason. "Activate Power Crystals—now! Let's show 'em Megazord Power!"

Two Zords locked into a third, *Clunk! Clang!* and became legs. Two more Zords locked in, *Clang! Thunk!* and formed arms.

The mighty head rose from its chest. Its helmet swung open and locked into place. Its shield clanged into its chest.

In moments the Dinozords had locked together to form the mighty Megazord!

Lights flashed on in the control room behind the Megazord's eyes. All five Power Rangers sat at the controls, ready for action.

"Come on, guys," said Jason. "Let's round up that horsey!"

Now the Power Rangers towered over the city of Angel Grove. The Polluticorn flew in for the first strike. The Megazord staggered, but refused to fall.

Then the Polluticorn landed on its clawed feet. It began to flap its huge wings. "Toxic wings, blow!" it cried.

Polluted hurricane-force winds blew across the landscape. Buildings shook. Huge trees ripped from the ground. Even the Megazord could not withstand its power. It tumbled backward through the air.

The ground shook as the Megazord landed. The Power Rangers looked at one another. It was time to call on greater power.

"We need the Power Sword!" Jason cried.

Instantly a huge sword sliced toward Earth. It locked into place in the Megazord's powerful hand. Raising the sword high, the Megazord rose in the air.

The Polluticorn froze. "Huh!? Uh-oh—" It began to back up as the Megazord flew toward it.

The Power Sword struck. The Polluticorn slammed to the ground. In a cloud of crackling electricity and a shower of fireworks and flames, it disappeared.

It was a good day on Earth. The Power Rangers had cleaned up their community. And they had defended the planet from Rita's evil plan.

"Aaaaghh!" Rita Repulsa cried, turning away from her telescope. Then she grabbed the sides of her head. "Those Power Rangers give me a headache!"

CHAPTER 6

Jason, Billy, Trini, Zack, and Kimberly were back in their jeans and T-shirts and hi-tops, waiting for science class to begin.

Ms. Appleby walked to the front of the room just as the bell rang. She smiled at her students as they took their seats, until her eyes fell on Bulk. Then her smile soured a little. "Today we'll be seeing Bulk and Skull's video. Won't we?"

Bulk looked around. Where is Skull? he thought. "Uh, well, I—"

Crash! The door banged open and Skull rushed into the room. He held up the videotape. "Just finished editing it!" he said.

Ms. Appleby looked doubtful. "This should be very interesting."

Bulk smiled nervously. "I'm sure it's an award-winning project." As Skull sat down, Bulk whispered, "How does it look?"

"A few glitches," Skull said. "But nothing to worry about."

Ms. Appleby started the video.

Soon the title appeared on the screen: *Bulk, the World's Greatest Guy*. Bulk grinned. A few girls in the class giggled.

But something was wrong. The tape was all jumpy. Scenes were mixed up. Words were chopped in half.

In the first classroom scene, Bulk seemed to say: *"I...have...no ...class. That Ms. Appleby... can't...teach...*

The whole class burst out laughing. Bulk's face turned bright red.

"H-hey," Skull stammered. "I-I thought I cut that out!"

Then they saw a scene of Bulk smashing into a tower of aluminum cans at the youth center recycling drive. His choppy edited voice seemed to say: *"I . . . should be recycled."*

Kimberly couldn't stop laughing. Ms. Appleby's body shook as she tried not to giggle.

Bulk exploded like a volcano. "I'M GONNA POUND YOU, CAMERAMAN!"

Skull jumped up out of his chair. The last thing the Power Rangers heard as Bulk chased Skull out of the room was, "I can fix it. I can fix it!"

Jason, Trini, Billy, Zack, and Kimberly grinned at one another. It had been a good week.

They were proud of their teamwork in cleaning up Angel Grove, and their teamwork in protecting the Earth from harm.

But it was great just to be hanging out again, having fun in class together. As if they were just regular kids.

Kids with a very big secret.